Why Don't Dogs Wear Shoes?

Jerry Chiappetta

PublishAmerica
Baltimore

© 2004 by Jerry Chiappetta.
All rights reserved. No part of this book may be reproduced, stored in a retrieval system or transmitted in any form or by any means without the prior written permission of the publishers, except by a reviewer who may quote brief passages in a review to be printed in a newspaper, magazine or journal.

First printing

ISBN: 1-4137-3238-0
PUBLISHED BY PUBLISHAMERICA, LLLP
www.publishamerica.com
Baltimore

Printed in the United States of America

Dedicated to Johnny, Kim, Angela, Ryan, Jenny, Ace, Jessie, Austin, Jake and Evan.

God appointed dogs as guardians for humans. When they walk beside us, fulfilling their doggie karmic mission as companion and protector, their four little feet move so fast that they are nearly invisible, never touching the ground for very long — no shoes required. Like true angels, they never really set foot on the earth long enough to need shoes.

—Unknown

The Third Phase

Life comes in three flavors or phases.

Phase I is roughly the first 25 years, when we grow up and learn about the opposite sex, snag a job, and create some digs of our own after being kicked out of momma's house.

Phase II is roughly the next 40 or so, years involving matrimony, maternity, mortgages, middle age, and monotony, plus a little fatherhood and motherhood thrown in to fill up our spare time.

Phase III is the period more and more of us are in these days, when the AARP crams our mailboxes with invitations to join and buy their insurance for seniors. How in the world do our names get onto so many snail mail, e-mail and junk spam lists? This is also the phase of life when we are most likely to become grandparents who can sing lullabies, read fairy tales, examine fascinating bugs, take long hikes with grandkids, share family history, and teach them about life.

We're the only ones in the grandkids' lives with time for all that. We're also the ones ready to give up our homes and friends to move across the country to where the grandkids are living. So let's take our Lipitor and high blood-pressure pills to make sure we'll be around for a long, loving relationship, as those grandkids grow and journey through life. Give them guidance starting with reading to them or, at least, introducing them to good stories and books.

A word of caution: We grandparents should not try to be parents again. Our grandkids' parents are the parents today. Work with these new parents, unless of course, there is some problem involving your grandchild's health or safety.

Don't meddle or criticize or try to raise our grandchildren like we raised our children. Heaven knows we screwed them up enough already. Let's not repeat those mistakes. Times and techniques of nurturing, feeding, teaching and doctoring have changed. Live with it.

Good grandparenting requires a conscious effort to prevent coming between grandkids and their parents. Our lives are going to be different. We'll have to buy a child's seat for our car, baby-proof our new place, and avoid shoving old baby furniture from the attic or resale shops onto the new parents in the family. Styles, materials, lead paint, placement of crib slats and recalls may have made our old infant furniture dangerously obsolete.

Grandparenting does not mean we can spoil the kids, bribe them with toys, candy and balloons and then take them home when they get naughty. That's a myth. Grandparents who try to bribe the little ones to win their affection and respect are on the wrong path. Shower them with love, not stuff.

Give them your time and attention because their parents are probably working long hours — sometimes two jobs — to make ends meet. With babies in the family, those *ends* seem to grow farther and farther apart. We should never disrespect our adult children in front of our new grandchildren. We may think we have more experience and are smarter, but don't embarrass or humiliate your adult children. We must not discredit their feelings and experiences just because we're older.

Grandparents have more time to listen to the little ones and discuss things with them like the little people they are. Explain things honestly and clearly, and as simply as possible using words they understand.

Just as cute, cuddly puppies grow up to become dogs, so do cute, cuddly little grandkids grow up to become teenagers who have to be treated differently. With grandchildren whose ages are measured in double numbers, we must become *with it* Grandpas and Grandmas or those grandkids won't be comfortable around us. In this teen stage, upgrade your activities. Try a major league ball game, cruise the mall, watch movies they like, and, when they're old enough, try wilderness hiking and camping, white-water rafting, horseback riding, and sightseeing in national parks. Teach them about nature and the great outdoors. Introduce them to hunting and fishing. Work in historic or educational angles during those big trips without being obviously historic or educational.

All things considered, grandparenthood will put new bounce in your step, new purpose in your life, and give you new responsibilities.

Following are some stories you can read aloud to your grandchildren. Of course, determine their level of comprehension and select the story or stories they might enjoy at bedtime or anytime.

—Jerry Chiappetta

Why Don't Dogs Wear Shoes?

A curly-headed four-year-old named Jacob jumped up on his Grandpa's lap, studied Grandpa's face and head and asked, "Papa, why is your hair all white?"

"Well, Jake, people change as they get older. My hair changed from brown to white," his Grandpa said.

"Why?" Jake asked.

"Things just do," his Papa said. "Things change. Like, we can't run as fast as we used to. Our muscles change."

"Why?"

"Because, well, we slow down," Papa said. "Sometimes our hearts don't beat as good and, our arms and legs aren't so strong anymore."

"Why?"

"Parts wear out…get run down," Jake's Papa continued.

"Oh," Jake said. "But why is your face falling off?"

"It's not falling off, Jake." Papa laughed. "I have a few wrinkles and a little sagging. That's all."

Jake flashed his Papa a frown.

"Remember that little fire truck we got you for your first birthday?" Papa asked. "You used to ride it all the time, but you're bigger now and can't ride it anymore. You've changed a little bit."

Jake nodded as if he understood, but he still looked a bit puzzled. Then, Jake's big blue eyes widened.

"When I get big, will my hair turn white and my face fall off too?" Jake asked.

"Not for a long, long, long time," Papa said. "Remember how the wheels on your little fire truck began to wobble and squeak?"

Jake nodded yes.

"It's the same thing," his Papa continued. "The wheels wore out, just like our bodies wear out a little bit at a time."

The topic was getting too serious for such a nice day and Jake was not quite old enough to understand much more about growing old. Jake was only four.

The boy gazed up at the sky for a moment, put a finger to his chin and with eyebrows arched in a sense of discovery, exclaimed, "I know! I know! When we were at the petting zoo, the farmer was changing shoes on his horse!"

"Exactly," Papa said, pleased that maybe he was getting through to his grandson. "Horseshoes wear out and have to be changed from time to time."

Jake thought about that for a second and a half, and asked the big question, "Why don't dogs wear shoes?"

"I never thought much about that, Jake," his Papa said. "Most dogs walk so fast, their little paws hardly touch the ground. I guess they don't need shoes."

"Why do horses need shoes?" Jake asked.

"That's a good question," his Papa said. "They have different kinds of hooves — feet that are soft. They're heavier and their feet — hooves — touch the ground more."

Fortunately, Jake didn't ask why again.

Lightning had knocked out the power the day before Jake came over for a visit. When Grandpa told Jake power was off in the house, Jake wanted to know, "Did Grandma use up all the 'lectricity?"

"No," Papa chuckled. "The thunderstorm interrupted service."

"Did the pipe break?" Jake asked.

"Not exactly." His Papa smiled.

"Did all the 'lectricity run out?" Jake asked.

It was obvious Jacob related the flow of 'lectricity to the flow of water. Months before that happened there had been a plumbing problem at Jake's house. Water from an overflowing toilet soaked through the floor and damaged ceiling tiles in their basement.

This reminded Grandpa of a story he was told when he was a little boy. Papa said that when he was about Jacob's age his older brother told him all homes had three power lines.

WHY DON'T DOGS WEAR SHOES?

"The top line was for new electricity going into the house. The bottom line was for the used electricity going back to the electricity factory and the third line was for birds to sit on."

Jake wrinkled up his nose.

"Let's take MoeMoe for a run," Papa said. MoeMoe was always ready for a hike through the woods near Grandfather's house. MoeMoe was Papa's constant companion, but he was also an *anti-hunting* bird-hunting dog despite American Kennel Club papers attesting to his pure pedigree. MoeMoe didn't like the noise of a shotgun, but he liked sniffing out and flushing gamebirds. This very handsome brown and white Brittany delighted in bounding through the woods and fields chasing butterflies, rabbits, squirrels or anything else that would run. However, on his first real hunting trip when the first Ringneck pheasant took off and the first shotgun went off, MoeMoe dashed off to Grandpa's sport utility vehicle, made a mighty leap from the ground and crashed headfirst into the tailgate window of the vehicle. Obviously, he did not realize the rear window had been closed.

He appeared more embarrassed than hurt.

"Elephants are the only animals that can't jump," Jake said as they strolled along watching MoeMoe dash from tree to tree sniffing for his *pee-mail*. Spotting on trees trunks and fence posts is a dog's way of leaving his signature, his mark so that other dogs would know who had passed this way earlier.

"You've been watching *Animal Planet*?" Papa laughed. "Let's keep going before it rains."

Along the trail some slobs had left a half dozen empty beer cans scattered around the playground swings and sandbox.

"Damn litterbugs!" Grandpa's muttered words were not meant for Jake to hear, but he did hear them.

"Damn litterbugs," Jake repeated. The boy repeated everything. "Do litterbugs live here and grow these cans?" Jake asked.

"Litterbugs are slobs," his Papa said. "They don't live out here to grow trash. They finish their drinks and chips and toss their trash on the ground instead of putting it in trash barrels. Disgusting."

"Litterbugs disgust me too," Jake scowled. "They make me sad. We should punch litterbugs in the nose and put them all in jail!"

"If we catch them, maybe we'll do that," Papa said. "For now, lets pick up these cans and put them in the barrel."

Jake and his Grandfather collected the aluminum cans and stomped them flat. Jake liked that, as though smashing the cans was some sort of revenge on the litterbugs. He caught his Papa totally off guard with another of his observations.

"Papa, litterbugs throw their smokerettes out here too," he said.

Smokerettes, Grandpa guessed were cigarette butts.

"Yep, Jake. They're extra bad," Papa said. "You could die from smokerettes."

"Papa, it is good that litterbugs are going to die from smokerettes," Jake announced.

"That's a bit harsh, Jake," Papa said.

Linking littering directly to smokerettes and death as a punishment was the way a four-year-old might think about it. Jake's Papa attempted to put it all in perspective, but was saved by the first drops of rain.

"Come on, little buddy, we have to hurry home," Papa said.

Jake wasn't happy about leaving the hiking trail and dashing back to the house. He wanted to ride the swings at the little playground.

"Jake, come on. It's starting to rain."

"Make it stop raining, Papa!"

Controlling the rain was a bit beyond Papa's range of grandfatherly abilities.

"Even Bob, the builder, couldn't do that."

Papa hoisted Jake up for a piggyback ride and called to MoeMoe to hurry along. They hustled back to Grandpa's garage before getting soaked.

"Make it stop raining, Papa," Jake pleaded. His lip quivered and tears welled up in his big blue eyes.

Grandpa unhooked a swing from a backyard play set and screwed a couple big hooks into the garage rafters. He opened the big garage doors to permit a nice summer breeze and was able to push Jake in the swing until the boy nodded off. Jake told everybody at dinner that evening, "Papa made it stop raining." He didn't explain this happened inside the garage, but his Papa took full credit anyway.

Jake was allowed to sleep over that night. Grandfather drove the boy to preschool the next day. Jake's teacher greeted them at the front door.

Grandfather said Jake was lucky to have another set of grandparents visiting from out of town.

"Where do your other grandparents live, Jacob?" his teacher asked.

"At the airport," he replied. "When we want to see 'em, we just go out to the airport and get 'em."

If it were not for Jacob, Papa would have never considered the question of "why don't dogs wear shoes" or that out-of-town grandparents all lived at the airport.

Grandpup Parenthood

Many grandpas and grandmas direct their love and attention toward pets once their children have moved away and before grandchildren become part of their lives — their new love sponges.

Of course, pets are a lot of fun, but before you run to the pound to adopt a pet, ponder this poop on pups.

Gracie, a little Brittany, was overdue in delivering her litter of puppies so she was taken to the neighborhood doggie doctor for a cesarean operation. A cesarean is when the doctor has to open up the mommy-dog's tummy to help the puppies be born. It doesn't hurt them because the mommy dog is asleep. That's what they tell us anyway.

Poor Gracie had "plumbing problems," according to the vet whose skills saved the day. The operation turned out to be a success and the vet helped Gracie deliver two beautiful females and a roly-poly little boy puppy. Grandpa called the puppies "rug rats" that crawled around by sheer will on little rubbery legs and rounded bellies. Their walking looked like they were swimming, like doing the breaststroke.

The three puppies were smaller than chipmunks — the perfect size for Yodi, Grandpa's Siamese cat, and his buddy, Sammy, another Siamese cat, who also thought he was a miniature mountain lion, not just another Siamese cat.

Grandpa and Grandma had to be constantly on guard to keep the cats from eating these very helpless puppies. Meanwhile, Momma Gracie was miffed over this whole motherhood thing. First, she suffered through an arranged marriage to a blue-ribbon prince charming named Duke whose reputation for romance was legend from here to Hawaii. Yes, Grandpa received a call from a man in Hawaii who wanted to buy one of Gracie's puppies after Duke's owner had put out the word she was expecting. You see, mother dogs have their puppies just sixty-three days after they get married to daddy dogs. That's nine weeks. Looking at it another way, that's two months and two days. In humans, gestation is nine months — or about 36 weeks.

Gracie awoke from her operation to find these cute little critters crawling all over her. Grandpa named them Lori, Moe and Shirley after the Three Stooges.

Gracie was a sourpuss who growled at her puppies when they tried to get at mother's milk. Grandpa guessed that Gracie's un-motherly attitude might have been caused by her operation or because she had been denied natural puppy birth. Her grouchiness also could have been due to the fact that her new husband never sent flowers or candy, and never called after their romantic interlude.

Grandma Rita cuddled Gracie and petted her gently to distract her so Grandpa could sneak around to stick the little pups on her swollen nipples where they slurped up mother's milk. Puppies need to feed every couple of hours, day and night. Grandma and Grandpa were very busy.

All the puppies wanted to do was eat, sleep, and poop — eat, sleep, and poop — eat, sleep, and poop — over and over and over.

Every couple hours, day and night, soft whimpering was heard coming from the whelping box. Such a box is like a puppy nursery, a deluxe affair with fluffy, warm blankets, a large hunting sock stuffed with a hot water bottle that required one minute and fifty-two seconds in the microwave, and freshly washed towels changed every hour or so by Grandma Rita. She also gave the puppies some toys, which, of course, they couldn't see. New puppies don't open their eyes until they are about ten days old. They find their mother by smell. Dogs have great noses and wonderful ability to sniff out things.

No matter where Momma Gracie went, the new puppies crawled to her as if guided by radar. They always managed to find Gracie who alternated between grooming and growling at them, but she was slowly getting used to the puppies and the idea of motherhood.

The day Grandpa dreaded had finally arrived. The puppies had to have their tails and dewclaws clipped. A friend who was an experienced dog breeder came over with his scissors, needle and thread and a pair of large nail clippers to whack off the excess puppy parts to complete the Brittany fashion statement. Brittanys have very short nubs for tails so they don't snag on briers when hunting. That is standard for the breed.

Fortunately, Gracie took to motherhood after the minor clippings and became very protective of her babies. A few nights after these little puppy operations, in Grandpa's downstairs office where he kept the whelping box, Gracie went nuts, howling and scratching at the glass doors of the fireplace.

Grandma Rita poked Grandpa in the ribs to wake him. It was the middle of the night.

"Get your gun. Go see what's wrong downstairs. Somebody might be breaking in."

With a BB gun in one hand and an old flashlight in the other, Grandpa waddled down the steps in his bathrobe. Sure enough, Gracie was jumping at the glass fireplace doors and barking like she had gone loco. No matter what command Grandpa gave her, she continued her rampage of barking and jumping against the fireplace doors.

"Take the puppies upstairs," Papa instructed Grandma Rita. "They're terrified by all this noise."

Grandma scooped the puppies up in her nightgown and took the tiny trio to the master bedroom. Gracie had to be restrained with her leash tied around the only thing nearby — a very large, heavy lamp on Grandpa's desk.

He cautiously opened the glass doors of the fireplace, crouched down on the brick hearth and leaned into the fireplace to get a look up the chimney. Of course, he couldn't see a thing because everything was black as midnight, but he could hear the scratching of claws of some critter up inside the metal flue.

"A raccoon! That's it," Grandpa announced. "A raccoon!"

What better, warmer place in winter than a chimney that is not in use? Winter is prime nesting time for wild 'coons. These nocturnal carnivores are chiefly gray, with black masks and bushy, ringed tails. They resemble little bandits who live mostly in trees, and have a varied diet of fruits, nuts, bird's eggs and small animals like little puppies.

Grandpa was sure one had come down the chimney and was sitting on the ledge out of sight up inside the fireplace above the logs.

I'll smoke him out, Grandpa thought. *Good idea!*

He stuffed crumpled up newspapers, which he grabbed from the whelping box, and stuffed them into the fireplace. A cloud of thick smoke billowed up through the chimney, but then reversed course to curl back into the room. The smoldering papers, stained with puppy poo and pee, smelled awful.

Gracie looked at Grandpa like he had gone loco too. She resumed barking as the smoke alarms blared in the office, the halls and the stairway. Grandma Rita yelled from the upstairs bedroom that it smelled like the house was on fire and she was going to call the fire department.

"Just hang on," Grandpa yelled up to her. "I've got things under control. You save the puppies."

Grandpa felt that having the fire department drive up with their big red fire truck in the middle of the night would have been as embarrassing as stopping to ask directions when only a little bit lost. The burning newspapers had set fire to a few rotten logs, which had been left on the iron grates. Those smoldering logs added their smoke and smell to the house. Grandpa, wearing a pair of work gloves, snatched up the logs and pitched them outside into a snow bank. They sizzled for a moment and went out.

Meanwhile, the open patio doors next to the fireplace sucked some of the smoke out of the office, but the screaming fire alarms were still doing their job. Grandma Rita again yelled from upstairs that Grandpa should do something quick because the puppies were crying. Gracie continued barking and pulling on her leash until she dragged the heavy lamp off the desk. When it hit the edge of the brick hearth, both bulbs popped and flashed like lightning, and the shade was ripped and ruined.

The entire downstairs was once again dark and now full of smoke.

"'Coons are famous disease carriers," Grandpa said to Gracie as if Gracie understood.

In the room next to Grandpa's office were a portable movie light and an old refrigerator where Grandpa kept film cold to preserve it. The fridge was also a good place to stick the noisy smoke alarms to shut them up. The freezer compartment worked best.

Grandpa looked silly. He had buckled a heavy battery belt over his bathrobe and turned on the photo light. The Sungun gave the room an eerie bluish look, thanks to the intensity of the 250-watt bulb and the smoke, which hung heavy in the air.

Grandpa found his BB gun on the floor and now was angry and embarrassed enough to use it. Armed again with the gun in one hand and the bright Sungun in the other, Grandpa nudged open the glass doors with his toes like a chimpanzee, took a deep breath and stuck his head into the fireplace for another look up the chimney.

It was still black as midnight in there and he couldn't see a thing. However, this time there was no noise from animal claws scratching on the metal flue. *Smoking the critter out must have worked*, he thought.

Grandpa had driven the masked invader from his castle and saved his family of puppies. In the morning, he called the village volunteer fire department. When the firemen installed wire mesh covers over chimneys they found raccoon tracks in the soot. No animal was going to get down Grandpa's chimney again unless he knew how to use heavy wire cutters.

Grandpa hoped that the toughest part of having new puppies had passed after that nighttime adventure. All he had to do from here on out was feed them, vet them, train them, hunt them, protect them, and love them for many happy years.

Grandpa's home was never the same again. He and Grandma warned visitors to watch their step, and that if they don't love animals they might want to stay away.

So, there they were with three new puppies, plus two adult Brittanys — Gracie and her aunt, Birdie — and two Siamese cats named Yodi and Sammy. The place was a happy zoo.

MoeMoe, the little male puppy, lived under Grandpa's desk to escape his female littermates who tormented him despite the fact that he was the largest of the pups. While his sisters just wanted to play, MoeMoe just wanted to sleep. That's what puppies do best.

Grandpa promised MoeMoe, as he rolled around on Grandpa's lap, that he would never give him away or sell him, and that MoeMoe would have a home there forever and ever. Grandpa and Grandma would be his protectors for all times. Puppies like MoeMoe understand everything you say to them. So, keep your promises and never lie.

The chubby little puppy licked Grandpa's face, nibbled on his ears and stole Grandpa's heart.

A Boy's Big Adventure

When you see a deer sneaking through the cedars, or a magnificent elk standing on a mountainside, or a trout scurrying over the polished pebbles of a stream, it makes you tingly all over.

Fascination with these and other such wild things began half a century ago on Grandpa's first deer hunt with his father and his uncle, Jimmy. Grandpa was a skinny teenager back then, as he trudged along in the pre-dawn darkness behind his father and uncle through a foot of fresh snow. Heavy flakes had fallen all night in those mountains of northern Pennsylvania. The moon was so bright the lad could see his own shadow on the snow. To the boy, the area seemed a vast wilderness filled with wonder and mystery although it was only farmland butting up to the edge of a state forest.

The cold air stung his lungs and his nostrils stuck together with each breath. However, he didn't dare complain. He huffed and puffed to keep up as they crossed the blue-white fields of snow heading toward the dark forest ahead on the horizon.

The boy's father had bundled him in layers of heavy clothing. His thick, itchy, red and black checked Woolrich coat weighed 20 pounds. The pockets were crammed with a couple salami sandwiches, two Hershey bars, a box of Smith Brothers cough drops, a king-sized Bowie knife, and two boxes of .35-Remington bullets. Slung over the boy's shoulder was a nine-pound rifle with a four-power telescopic sight. It was so big and the boy was so small, the stock of the rifle sometimes dragged in the snow.

Fast-moving snow clouds blotted out the moon from time to time, but once they passed, the eerie blue light of the pre-dawn returned. Winds picked up, driving new snow sideways into the boy's face and he had to squint to keep it from stinging his eyes. He could only see a few yards in any direction.

The lad was operating on pure excitement, stretching hard to fit his steps into his father's boot tracks. He couldn't use his flashlight because it would alert the deer, his father had told him when they first left their car in the farmer's yard.

The boy's father was a tough steel-mill worker who struggled to raise nine children. Money was tight. Life was tough. But deer hunting was a special time in the family when The Old Man mellowed.

"Doctors and dentists are a bunch of crooks," the boy's father used to say. Once he pulled one of his own aching teeth with a pair of pliers rather than go to a dentist. He was a tough guy who climbed giant smoke stacks at the mill to chip rust and repaint the stacks. However, when deer season rolled around, he was a totally different person.

For weeks prior to hunting, there would be long evenings for the telling and retelling of hunting stories around the kitchen table with an assortment of hunting pals. The boy ate it up. It was his passage to manhood, like a Maasi youth sent out onto the African plains to hunt down a lion with nothing but courage and a spear.

The father allowed this son to skip a few days of school to go hunting. The Old Man wasn't much on reading books or magazines or studying the ways of wildlife. He used to say you learned by doing. For example, he swore if he reached his favorite deer runway in the dark and sat like a statue on a certain mossy stump he would shoot a buck. His tactic usually worked thanks to his hunter's eye, quick reflexes and stoic ability to remain absolutely silent and motionless for hours despite biting, cold winds and stinging sleet and snow.

Uncle Jimmy, on the other hand, was younger and more nervous about his hunting. They called him "a directional hunter." He took the ribbing as a good sport. He was full of "sure-fire" tactics that proved not to be so sure-fire. He would "stalk 'em up," "walk 'em down," "circle 'em in the swamp," or "come in from the east when the wind blew from the west."

No one could recall Uncle Jimmy ever bringing home venison, yet he brought back great stories in which he blamed misfiring ammo, snow-clogged sights, frozen rifle actions, fog in the 'scope or some other excuse for not connecting. Of course, this meant he had to trade in this year's rifle for another new one. He was also so cheap he wouldn't use good hunting ammunition to zero-in his new hunting rifles.

The boy, his father and his uncle trudged along for what seemed like an hour through the snow that opening morning to reach their "secret spots." The Old Man told the boy to be still, to stand guard under a large pine tree that had long, swooping branches that offered some protection from the heavy snowfall.

The two adults hiked a little farther along a pipeline to their pre-selected stands, the ones they had used for many past seasons. The father told the boy, "Look hard for antlers before shooting, and don't wander around and get lost."

You could bet money on that last part. The young hunter, a little frightened about being left alone in the dark, wasn't about to go more than an arm's length from his stand against the huge pine tree.

The falling snows had eased and the boy's eyes had adjusted to the gloom, the darkest time before first light. Against the fresh snow, he convinced himself, it would be easy to see a bear or a mountain lion or a wild cat or any other critter sneaking up behind him, he imagined, to kill and eat him.

He kicked away the snow at the base of the pine so he could turn without the snow squeaking under his four-buckle Arctic boots. Surprisingly, his feet were warm. In fact, he had worked up a lot of body heat from their long trek across the wide fields and into the forest. He had on two pairs of heavy wool socks and a pair of oversized bedroom slippers stuffed inside his rubber boots. He shoved his cold hands down inside his two pairs of blue jeans and long johns to transfer a little of that body heat to his frozen fingers. He had to go to the bathroom, but he did not dare move.

Despite an imagination working overtime, he could not transform any of the stumps, fence posts or fallen branches into a buck deer, a bear or any other critter. Around 7 a.m., there were a few distant gunshots, but otherwise action was slow for an opening morning in Pennsylvania, which boasted about a million deer hunters.

The boy ate half a salami sandwich and a chocolate bar before the sun sneaked up and over the mountain and lit up the treetops. That's when he heard a rifle shot very close, a pause and then six quick popping pistol cracks. The gunshots startled him. He stopped in mid-chew and slipped his half-eaten sandwich back into his pocket without rewrapping it.

That's got be Uncle Jimmy, he thought. He has a .38 S&W revolver to back up his .300 Savage rifle. The Smith & Wesson was inadequate as a weapon to shoot a deer, but Uncle Jimmy, who fashioned himself as a modern-day Gene Autry, felt good about carrying it.

These thoughts raced through the boy's head, *What do I do now? Move? Stay put? Take off the safety? Hold my rifle up at the ready?*

The lad stood motionless, unblinking, and looking hard in the direction the shots had come from, beyond what appeared to be a solid wall of evergreens. Through the snow-covered pines, a tawny brown form materialized about 15 yards away. It turned into a deer as big as a horse with great ears, a black nose blowing steam and a white tail up like a flag. It stopped dead in its tracks and stared right at the boy. Then the big deer silently loped past, almost close enough for the boy to touch it. The boy was stunned by the size and beauty of the animal and still could not move a muscle. He just stood there for a few more moments. It seemed as of the entire world had gone into slow motion.

The boy's trance was broken when his Uncle Jimmy came through the thick wall of snow-covered evergreen trees on the deer's trail.

"Why didn't you shoot?" Uncle Jimmy scolded.

"No horns," the boy fibbed.

"It was a spike," Uncle Jimmy insisted. "Spikes are legal."

"He was running too fast," the boy fibbed again.

Uncle Jimmy knelt down to examine of the tracks following their whispered exchange.

"Maybe I hit him," he said. "Help me look for blood."

The boy followed his uncle and the deer's prints in the fresh snow, but there was no blood and he was happy about that. Then, from another direction, they heard a single loud shot that shattered the silence.

"That's your Old Man," Uncle Jimmy exclaimed. "Hot dog! I bet he got one."

They hurried through the thick pines, backtracking to where they discovered the boy's father standing over the biggest buck that ever lived; bigger than the Hartford stag, a dead monster with its tongue sticking out of the side of its mouth and its eyes already glassed over. It was a nine-pointer with thick, heavy antler beams. The boy had to look away during the field dressing operation, but when it was completed, he knelt down and petted the swollen neck of the buck.

The remainder of the boy's first week of hunting was not nearly as exciting as that first morning on this big adventure. They never found Uncle Jimmy's mysterious spike buck. At the conclusion of the two-week buck season, there was a two-day doe season for antlerless whitetails. Uncle Jimmy was by the boy's side when several deer ran down a valley directly toward them. Uncle Jimmy coached the boy to pick out a big doe and shoot.

WHY DON'T DOGS WEAR SHOES?

Four nervously fired shots brought down the doe. A final shot was needed. The boy cried over the deer although he tried unsuccessfully to hide his tears. He would remain forever grateful to his Uncle Jimmy who field dressed the deer for him. Sensitive to the lad's feelings, Uncle Jim never teased him or spoke of his tears to the Old Man. And, the boy never told Uncle Jimmy or anybody else that while walking across those snow-swept fields heading back to their car at the conclusion of the earlier buck hunt, several deer bounded out ahead of them. They were beautiful wild things.

Tears rolled down his father's leathery face. They never mentioned that to each other or anyone else. It remained their secret for more than half a century.

The boy's father and Uncle Jimmy are gone now, but every deer season the boy has a salami sandwich in their honor and replays all those wonderful visions of all those wonderful wild things they helped him discover.

That's what hunting means to that boy who is now Jake's Grandpa.

Fast forward 50 years. Today that boy is a sixty-something Grandpa and his grandson, Jake, is with him as Grandpa packs for another hunting trip.

Little Jake asks, "Why do you go hunting?"

"I'll explain it sometime," Papa says. "I've got to get going now to meet the others in our hunting group."

Jake's simple question — "Why hunt?" — rang in Grandpa's ears all week as the hunter leaned back against a tree. He shivered on stand with a rifle cradled in his arms. The trees groaned and swayed in five-degree weather as a 20-mile-per-hour wind howled through naked branches. It was very cold with a wind chill that made it feel well below zero.

Why go hunting? was a tough question, but Grandpa had time to think about it. His hunting area was not far from the location of his first hunt with his father and Uncle Jimmy long ago.

Reasons to hunt are many — probably as many as there are hunters, Grandpa thinks. *How could a little boy comprehend all of our reasons to go hunting, something embedded in a man's genes, in his soul?*

How could little Jake possibly understand that hunting is important to control the size of the deer herd? How could shooting a deer be better than killing it with a car, or letting it starve in the winter cold and snow or die from diseases or overcrowding? If there are too many deer, they can't get enough food to survive in winter when they need nourishment the most.

How could anyone — except a wildlife biologist or other serious student of nature — appreciate the fact that harvesting some animals is good for the herd as a whole?

Reasons to hunt are hard to put into simple words for anyone to understand, let alone a little boy like Jake.

Grandpa tried to put all those ideas into words when he returned home and Jake came over for a visit. But, by the look on Jake's face, Grandpa doubted he was getting through to him. He thought about explaining that venison is healthy food, much better than a "Happy Meal" from McDonald's, but he didn't go down that road. When Jake gets a little older, Grandpa promised himself, he would talk to him about the tingly feeling one gets when you see a whitetail deer sneaking through the big woods.

Grandpa's strong personal reason for hunting was tradition, the gathering of family members and friends in some tent or cabin or old shack back in the pines, back in the past.

When Grandpa asked one of his brothers why he hunted, his brother said he hunted because it was something he had to do away from home.

Jake and Grandpa, like many city residents, often spotted deer in the backyard, in suburban parks and woodlots and on the edge of town or around local farms and nurseries.

"Backyard deer — city deer — are not the same as the wild ones we hunt in the big woods," Grandpa told Jake. "Wild deer are different from those fearless critters eating Grandma's flowers and shrubs along the back fence."

Everyone is sad to see deer killed by vehicles because it is such a waste of a beautiful animal. Hundreds of thousands of deer around the nation are killed on highways each year and countless thousands of others are hurt and crawl off to die in the woods out of sight. In addition, many motorists and their passengers are injured or killed in deer-car crashes, and there are millions and millions of dollars lost in vehicle damage.

Jake enjoyed hearing of the adventures of Grandpa's early hunting experience many years ago when his father and Uncle Jim let him tag along behind them in the dark forests and deep snows of northern Pennsylvania.

Maybe someday, Jake and other youngsters will understand why people hunt and appreciate the importance of hunting, and might want to join their fathers and grandfathers outdoors.

Things Grandpa Knows for Sure: Real Stories About Real Wildlife

The best way to get a youngster hooked on life in the real world, the outdoor world and not the cartoon world or the Hollywood world where animals talk like humans, is to expose kids to the outdoors early.

"Cartoon and movie animals" show lions and tigers and bears as cute and cuddly. They curl up to nap next to smaller animals like bunnies, squirrels, cats and puppies. In the real world, lions and tigers and bears consider those little critters *lunch*.

Mother Nature can often be cruel. She makes the winters cold and the snows deep. When food becomes scarce, a mother deer — a doe — will fight off its own fawns when competing for something to eat. Hollywood movies often give a different picture, a false picture that paints life in the wild as idyllic.

Unfortunately this is not reality, but Grandpa decided Jake needed a few more years of growing up before he went deeper into this discussion. He did tell the boy that when he thought he knew how wildlife might react, these critters often did something very different.

Here's what Grandpa thought he knew for sure about wildlife, the outdoors, and his hunting and fishing pals. Consider these examples:

- When out hunting, Grandpa can sit perfectly still for exactly 19 minutes. Squirrels can sit perfectly still for 20.
- Grandpa is always early. His hunting pals are always late.
- A friend's long shot was dumb luck. Grandpa's was skill.
- A hunting partner with an extra candy bar is hard to find.
- Wool coat sleeves are never so scratchy as when Grandpa's nose is dripping.

- Fish always hit lures Grandpa doesn't have in his tackle box.
- Barbed wire fences are always two inches higher than Grandpa's legs are long.
- The last hill before reaching the hunting cabin and is always the steepest.
- Deer are full-time animals. We are part-time hunters.
- Game and fish never weighed make for the best stories later.
- Outdoor pals always grab the check at the cheapest greasy-spoon cafes.
- Grandpa is always stuck with the check at the swankiest joints.
- The biggest gang of neighbors always appears when Grandpa drives up with the smallest deer.
- Grandpa's hunting dog, MoeMoe, always forgets all the wonderful things he was taught when the grandkids come over and Grandpa wants to show him off.
- Grandpa can never shoot as far as indicated in outdoor magazine advertisements for ammo; just as software Grandpa buys for his computer does not operate as easily as the ads say.
- Local newspapers never cover subjects Grandpa cares about.
- Mayonnaise is never good for sandwiches in your hunting coat.
- Deer aren't so smart; we're just dumber.
- Deer are somewhere all the time. Grandpa is too, but he calls it being lost.
- Hip boots always leak in the coldest duck marshes.
- If Grandpa wants the real lowdown on wildlife management, he asks his barber.
- Friends who give Grandpa the most advice, bring home the least amount of fish and game.
- Hunting and fishing were always better yesterday.
- Grouse hunting is always better next week when the leaves are down.
- Grandpa always get itchy when somebody in the gang finds a tick.
- Running after the hounds is hard work.
- No matter how strong your gun case, the airlines always damage your best firearms.
- No matter how many pairs of socks Grandpa puts on, his feet still freeze.

WHY DON'T DOGS WEAR SHOES?

- Grandma sleeps soundest when MoeMoe has to be let out on cold mornings.
- Grandkids are never watching when Grandpa does something good.
- Grandkids are always watching when Grandpa screws up.
- Grandpa's thermos always runs dry before he finishes his sandwiches in the woods.
- Sportsman's club dinners are tasty, but always bad for your health.
- Rocks always grow up out of the ground under Grandpa's sleeping bag after he is zipped in.
- Buddies always offer to buy gas on shortest trips.
- No matter how many extras on Grandpa's 4x4, his brother-in-law has more and bought his vehicle for less.
- No matter how short and sweet Grandpa's story is, his editor always wants to cut something important.

Update on Killing Time and Not Getting Caught During Phase III

There are many creative ways to spend time in Phase III of life with your grandchildren, especially teenaged grandkids who have high-tech minds. The trick is to learn to waste time without getting caught by Grandma.

Grandpa recently bought a new 800 mHz iMac computer, which is so speedy he can waste time faster than ever before.

Getting a pet is also high on the list of fun things to do. At one point, Grandpa had three Brittanys and two Siamese cats. Cleaning a litter box makes a good hobby. But, beware. There is a very fine line between hobby and mental illness, according to writer Dave Barry.

Breeding dogs is another good pastime, but could cause problems. If you mated a bulldog and a shih-tzu, would the offspring be called a *bullshih-tzu?* Stuff like that worries Grandpa.

Here's something else to worry about when wasting time; why do people point to their wrist for the time, but not to their crotch when they need to know where the toilet is?

In Grandpa's own imaginary state of Pleasantville, there is plenty of time to think about such things.

Grandpa was telling one of his grandchildren (he can't remember that one's name) about the days when "color" television meant sticking strips of colored plastic across the front of the black and white picture tube. It made the top third sky blue, the midsection reddish and the bottom-third green as grass — perfect for programs with scenes of fire trucks running across someone's lawn on blue-sky, sunny days.

Grandpa was stumped by the question, "Who was the first person to look at a cow and say, 'I think I'll squeeze these dangly things down there and drink whatever comes out?'"

He was probably the same guy who was the first to eat a snail and call it escargot. Another grandkid asked about favorite fast food when Grandpa was growing up.

"We didn't have fast food when I was growing up," he said. "All food was slow food."

"C'mon," he scowled. "Seriously, Papa, where did you eat?"

"At home," he said. "Grandma cooked every day and when Grandpa got home from the mill, we sat around the kitchen table and ate. No TV. Just food and family. If you didn't like what Grandma put on your plate, you were allowed to sit there until you did like it."

He didn't try to explain that Great Grandpa would toss a chunk of bread to his daughters, but would pass bread to his sons. He used to say he did that because when you give bread to girls, you never expected to get it back, but your sons will return it someday. It was an Italian thing that drove my Great Grandma nuts.

There were some other things Grandpa recalled about his childhood.

His parents never owned their own house, wore Levis, set foot on a golf course, traveled out of Pennsylvania or had a credit card. In later years, he recalled, they had a revolving charge good only at Sears & Roebuck. That was when there was Sears & Roebuck. There's no Roebuck anymore.

"I think he died or was bought out," Grandpa said.

His parents never drove to soccer practice. They never heard of soccer. Grandpa was twelve before he tasted a pizza back when it was called "pizza pie." Pizzas were not delivered, but milk was. It came in glass bottles with round cardboard caps. These would rise up on winter days and there would be two inches of pure cream sticking up out of the top of a quart bottle. On Grandpa's very first trip to the mountains, he saw a small deer before dawn on the porch of a home in northern Pennsylvania licking this cream from a bottle of milk.

The only phone in the house was in the living room where the kids slept on several beds pushed together next to a pullout sofa. Grandpa's first phone had no dial or push buttons and was on a party line. Before you could make a call, you had to listen to make sure people you didn't know weren't already using the line. You picked it up and talked to a live person.

Grandpa and a school friend conspired to call five minutes past six one evening to make a big impression on everyone that Grandpa was getting a telephone call, his first ever.

Newspapers were delivered by boys, and all boys delivered newspapers. Grandpa delivered *The McKeesport Daily News*. It cost a nickel a paper, of which delivery boys got to keep two cents. Saturday was collection day when most customers would not answer their doors. Grandpa worked all summer to earn $13.75. His mom chipped in the difference and bought him a $25.00 War Bond.

Back to killing time, try raising kittens.

One three-year-old came over to see a new litter of kittens. On returning home, he breathlessly informed his mother, "There were two boy kittens and two girl kittens."

"How did you know that?" she asked.

"Grandpa picked them up and looked underneath. I think it's printed on the bottom if they are boys or girls."

Of course, you can do something more productive than merely wasting time in Phase III of life. You can volunteer.

When Grandpa delivered hot meals to elderly shut-ins, he took his four-year-old grandkid with him on his rounds. Appliances used by the elderly such as their canes, walkers and wheelchairs intrigued the boy. One day, I caught him staring at a set of false teeth soaking in a glass.

He turned and whispered, "The tooth fairy will never believe this!"

Puppies make you feel good, especially when they lick your face and crawl all over you and nibble at your earlobes. Puppies also force you to get outdoors and walk, even when you don't want to. You have to take that puppy outdoors or clean up the mess in the house.

Walking is good for you. And you can take the grandkids along because it teaches them responsibility. Puppies also listen to all of your stories without complaint. You can talk to them all day and if you keep a nice tone to your voice, they never complain.

Get a puppy. Be happy. Enjoy your life.

Update on Language

Older grandkids in the teen range have developed their own language. Here are some of the same reasons why English is so tough for a lot of us older folks. Consider —

- The bandage was wound around the wound.
- The farm was used to produce produce.
- The dump was so full that it had to refuse more refuse.
- We must polish the Polish furniture.
- He could lead if he would get the lead out.
- The soldier decided to desert his dessert in the desert.
- Since there is no time like the present, he thought it was time to present the present.
- A bass was painted on the head of the bass drum.
- When shot at, the dove dove into the bushes.
- I did not object to the object.
- The insurance was invalid for the invalid.
- There was a row among the oarsmen about how to row.
- They were too close to the door to close it.
- The buck does funny things when the does are present.
- A seamstress and a sewer fell down into a sewer line.
- The farmer taught his sow to help with sowing.
- The wind was too strong to wind the sail.
- After a number of injections my jaw got number.
- Upon seeing the tear in the painting, I shed a tear.
- I had to subject the subject to a series of tests.
- How can I intimate this to my most intimate friend?

- There is no egg in eggplant, no ham in hamburger, no apple nor pine in a pineapple, and no crab in a crabapple.
- English muffins weren't invented in England.
- French fries (once called Freedom Fries) were invented in America.
- Sweetmeats are candies while sweetbreads, which aren't sweet, are meat.

Consider these paradoxes —

- Quicksand can work slowly.
- Boxing rings are square.
- A guinea pig is neither from Guinea nor is it a pig.
- Why is it that writers write but fingers don't fing, grocers don't groce and hammers don't ham?
- If the plural of tooth is teeth, why isn't the plural of booth beeth?
- If one is a goose, and two are geese, and one is a moose, why aren't two called meese?
- One index, two indices? Doesn't it seem crazy that you can make amends but not one amend?
- If you have a bunch of odds and ends and get rid of all but one of them, what do you call it?
- If teachers taught, why don't preachers praught?
- If a vegetarian eats vegetables, what does a humanitarian eat?

Sometimes I think all the English speakers should be committed to an asylum for the verbally insane.

In what other language do people recite at a play and play at a recital?

We ship by truck and send cargo by ship.

If your nose runs and your feet smell, are you built upside down? (Explain that one to your grandkids.)

How can a slim chance and a fat chance be the same, while a wise man and a wise guy are opposites?

You have to marvel at the lunacy of a language in which your house can burn up as it burns down, in which you fill in a form by filling it out and in which an alarm goes off by going on.

People, not computers, invented English and it reflects the creativity of the human race, which, of course, isn't a race at all.

WHY DON'T DOGS WEAR SHOES?

Doesn't the rush hour have the slowest moving traffic?

That is why when the stars are out, they are visible, but when the lights are out, they are invisible.

Punctuation? That's another :!?/# subject!

More points to ponder —

- If Webster wrote the first dictionary, where did he find the words?
- Why is the third hand on the watch called the second hand?
- If a word is misspelled in the dictionary, how would we ever know?
- Is it good if a vacuum really sucks?
- Why do we say something is out of whack? What is whack?
- Why do "slow down" and "slow up" mean the same thing?
- Why do tug boats push barges instead of tugging them?
- Why do we sing "Take me out to the ball game" when we are already there?
- Why are they called "stands" when they are made for sitting?
- Why is it called "after dark" when it really is "after light?"
- Why is phonics not spelled the way it sounds?
- If work is so terrific, why do they have to pay you to do it?
- If all the world is a stage, where is the audience sitting?
- If love is blind, why is lingerie so popular?
- If you are cross-eyed and have dyslexia, can you read all right?
- Why is bra singular and panties plural?
- Why do we press harder on the buttons of a remote control when we know the batteries are dead?
- Why do we put suits in garment bags and garments in a suitcase?
- Why do we wash bath towels? Aren't we clean when we use them?
- Why doesn't glue stick to the inside of the bottle?
- Why do they call it a TV set, when you only get one?

Gripers and the Gripies

When young people have a problem they complain or gripe about it. The same holds true for the people who fly big airplanes and other people who have to fix them.

Airline pilots fill out a *gripe sheet* after every flight to report problems to the airplane mechanics. Mechanics are supposed to fix the problems, and then respond in writing on what remedial action was taken. That means the mechanics have to fix the problems and then put it in writing as to what they did. Pilots review the gripe sheet before their next flight.

Here are actual maintenance complaints submitted by Qantas Airline pilots and the solutions offered by their aircraft mechanics. By the way, as of this writing, Qantas was the only major airline that has never had an accident.

(P = Stands for the problem logged by the pilot.)
(S = Indicates the solution.)

P: Left inside main tyre (cq) almost needs replacement.
S: Almost replaced left inside main tyre.

P: Test flight OK, except auto-land very rough.
S: Auto-land not installed on this aircraft.

P: Something loose in cockpit.
S: Something tightened in cockpit.

P: Dead bugs on windshield.
S: Live bugs on back-order.

WHY DON'T DOGS WEAR SHOES?

P: Autopilot in altitude-hold mode produces a 200 feet per minute descent.
S: Cannot reproduce this problem on the ground.

P: Evidence of leak on right main landing gear.
S: Evidence removed.

P: DME (Distance Measuring Equipment) volume unbelievably loud.
S: DME volume set to more believable level.

P: Friction locks cause throttle levers to stick.
S: That's what they are there for.

P: IFF inoperative.
S: IFF always inoperative in OFF mode.

P: Suspected crack in windshield.
S: Suspect you're right.

P: Number 3 engine missing.
S: Engine found on right wing after brief search.

P: Aircraft handles funny.
S: Aircraft warned to straighten up, fly right, and be serious.

P: Target radar hums.
S: Reprogrammed target radar with lyrics.

P: Mouse in cockpit.
S: Cat installed.

P: Noise coming from under instrument panel. Sounds like a midget pounding on something with a hammer.
S: Took hammer from midget.

These flying reports reminded Grandpa of earlier days when he was a pilot whose adventures still cause some giggles and shivers.

Grandpa radioed the tower at Pontiac, Michigan, one nasty winter day to find out how low the clouds were so he could fly in and make a safe landing. Grandpa called on his aircraft radio and asked, "What's the ceiling at Pontiac?"

A young woman in the control tower announced, "Acoustical tile."

Must be a trainee, Grandpa thought.

On landing that day, the tower then radioed Grandpa in his little Cessna for a *Pi-rep* on runway conditions. A *Pi-rep* is *FAA speak* for a pilot report on real-time conditions.

Jet jockeys flying airliners and large corporate aircraft often give Pi-reps on winds, icing conditions at various altitudes, thunderstorms, lightning, and other meteorological conditions that may affect another pilot's flight safety. Pi-reps are extremely important to the FAA, the weather bureau and to other pilots.

On this freezing, winter day, the tower asked Grandpa, "Cessna November-3-3-7-Zero-Tango how about a pi-rep on the icing conditions of runway 2-7? Over."

"Roger," Grandpa radioed back and paused to collect his thoughts.

Imagine, Grandpa thought as he taxied off of active runway 2-7, *Uncle Sam sitting way up there in that glass tower needs help from me, a lowly, new private pilot, on the ice and snow conditions on this main runway! What I announce in the next few seconds may prevent accidents and save women and children from death in a skidding aircraft. My info might aid the pilot of a mercy flight taking off with a heart in an Igloo cooler destined for a patient in some far-off city. Some poor soul could be awaiting a lifesaving transplant. Life and death are riding on my words, in my hands!*

Grandpa was swept up with the importance of what he was about to tell the tower. Trembling nervously in view of this overwhelming responsibility thrust upon him, he reached for the microphone.

Carefully, deliberately, he removed the mike from its cradle, took a deep breath, squeezed the button and announced with the deepest, most official-sounding pilot's voice he could muster. "Pontiac Tower, this is Cessna November-3-3-7-Zero-Tango, glad to be of service. We are reporting runway 2-7 at Pontiac is slippery on the icy spots and offers good traction on the bare concrete. Over."

There was a long pause.

"That's a fine roger, roger, Cessna November-3-3-7-Zero-Tango," came the tower's response with what sounded like laughter in the background.

"Glad to be of service," Grandpa said proudly, looking up and waving to those in the tower. With that, he taxied into a pile of slush and became bogged down in the mud at the turnoff to his parking area. No amount of gunning of the little 150-horsepower engine could free Cessna November-3-3-7-Zero-Tango. It was stuck.

"Pontiac ground control," Grandpa whispered into the mike, "can you call me a tow truck?"

"No sweat, Seven-Zero-Tango. Glad to be of service."

Perks of Unknown Origin

A perk is anything that is special, fun, surprising, or a gift received for no special reason. Here are some perks we can enjoy just for being Grandparents:

- Kidnappers are not very interested in us.
- In a hostage situation, we're released first.
- No one expects us to run into a burning building to save fire victims.
- People call at 10 a.m. and ask, "Did I wake you?"
- People no longer view us as hypochondriacs.
- There is nothing left to learn the hard way.
- Things we buy now will never wear out.
- We can eat dinner at 4 p.m.
- We can live without sex but not without our glasses.
- We enjoy hearing about other people's operations.
- We get into heated arguments about pension plans.
- We have a party and the neighbors don't realize it.
- We no longer think of speed limits as a challenge.
- We quit trying to hold our stomach in, no matter who walks into the room.
- We sing along with elevator music.
- Our eyes won't get much worse.
- Our investment in health insurance is finally paying off.
- Our joints are more accurate meteorologists than the Weather bureau.
- Our secrets are safe with our friends because they can't remember them either, and we can't remember where we got this list.

WHY DON'T DOGS WEAR SHOES?

Here are some games for Grandpas and Grandmas:

- Sag, you're it.
- Pin the toupee on the bald guy.
- Twenty questions shouted into your good ear.
- Kick the bucket.
- Red Rover, Red Rover, the nurse says Bend Over.
- Doc Goose.
- Simon says something incoherent.
- Hide and go pee.
- Spin the Bottle of Mylanta.
- Musical recliners.

Signs of menopause:

1. We sell our home heating system at a yard sale.
2. We write post-it notes with grandkids' names on them.
3. (We forgot #3.)
4. The Phenobarbital dose that wiped out the Heaven's Gate cult gives us four hours of decent rest.
5. We change our underwear after every sneeze.
6. Grandma is on so much estrogen that she takes her Brownie troop on a field trip to Chippendale's.

This makes grandchildren chuckle:

OLD IS WHEN ... Your friends compliment you on your new alligator shoes and you're barefoot.

OLD IS WHEN ... A sexy woman catches your fancy and your Pacemaker triggers the garage door opener.
OLD IS WHEN ... Going braless pulls the wrinkles out of Grandma's face.
OLD IS WHEN ... You don't care where your wife goes, just as long as you don't have to go along.
OLD IS WHEN ... You are cautioned to slow down by the doctor instead of by the police.
OLD IS WHEN ... "Getting a little action" means you don't need to take extra fiber today.
OLD IS WHEN ... "Getting lucky" means you can find your car in the parking lot.
OLD IS WHEN ... An all-nighter means not getting up to pee.

🐾 🐾

Senior citizens are always criticized for every conceivable deficiency in the modern world, real or imagined. However, we like to tell the grandkids senior citizens did not take:
The melody out of music,
The pride out of appearance,
The courtesy out of driving,
The romance out of love,
The love out of sex,
The commitment out of marriage,
The responsibility out of parenthood,
The togetherness out of the family,
The learning out of education,
The service out of patriotism,
The Golden Rule from rulers,
The nativity scene out of cities,
The civility out of behavior,
The refinement out of language,
The dedication out of employment,
The prudence out of spending,
The ambition out of achievement, and
God out of our government and our schools.

WHY DON'T DOGS WEAR SHOES?

🐾 🐾

As long as we're at it, how about:
You know you're a senior if —

- You're the life of the party even if it lasts until 8 p.m.
- You're very good at opening childproof caps with a hammer.
- You're usually interested in going home before you get to where you're going.
- You're awake many hours before your body allows you to get up.
- You're smiling all the time because you can't hear a thing anybody is saying.
- You're very good at telling stories — over and over and over and over.
- You're aware that other people's grandchildren are not nearly as cute as your own.
- You're so cared for — long-term care, assisted-living care, nursing-home care, eye care, home care, dental care, etc.
- You're not really grouchy, you just don't like traffic, waiting, crowds, lawyers, loud music, other people's unruly grandkids, Toyota commercials, Peter Jennings, Tom Brokaw, or Dan Rather, barking dogs, politicians and a few other things you can't remember right now.
- You're sure everything you can't find is in a safe secure place somewhere.
- You're wrinkled, saggy, lumpy, and that's just your left leg.
- You're having trouble remembering simple words like dahhhhh…
- You're beginning to realize that aging is not for wimps.
- You're sure they are making adults much younger these days, and when did they let kids become policemen and doctors and dahhhhh…?
- You're wondering, if you're only as old as you feel, how could you be alive at 150? And, how can your grandkids be older than you feel sometimes?
- You're a walking storeroom of facts. You've just lost the key to the storeroom.

A Dog's Life
by
MoeMoe

My name is MoeMoe. I'll just sit here looking cute and stare out the patio door until Grandpa over there receives my telepathic message that can't be ignored forever.

I have rights, you know!

If something doesn't happen soon, I'll contact the NAACP, NASA, NSA, NRA, NBC, NPR, SPCA or one of those other alphabetical organizations to file a complaint against my man.

Let's get a few things straight before I go on.

I'm from the province of Brittany in France. And, I'm good. Just look at my reflection in the window. Man, I am beautiful. Look at those huge brown eyes, my trim figure, sensitive, hot, moist lips; firm limbs and everything else in just the right place.

All around, anyway you look at it, I'm a blue-ribbon beauty. At least I've overheard other men saying so. I don't like being ignored like this. After all, we do share a bed and I do deserve some special attention.

But, all he does is sit there and bang on that darn keyboard over and over and over. He's driving me nuts. Nothing ever comes of it either. Look at him. His fat fingers thump recklessly across the keys, stumble here and there, and force him to use delete and backspace a lot. Without his spellchecker, he'd be nothing.

I can read his mind and know what he's thinking:

You're insensitive to my needs, too. I give you everything — a warm bed, a roof over your head, food, water, expensive leather playthings, strolls in the

WHY DON'T DOGS WEAR SHOES?

woods and occasional exotic country trips where we see lots of wildlife. Isn't that enough?

That may be what he's thinking, but I've got more on my mind.

"One more minute, my little French lovely," Grandpa says out loud. He tosses me a glance and returns to his typing.

"Just another sentence," he says. "Just another paragraph. Just another page, and I'll be done and have some time for you, my pet."

Yeah. That's what he says, but the keys keep on clicking. Why does he do it? He'll never sell that book anyway.

I might try huffing some steamy breath on the door glass to show him how hot I am? Or maybe I should swagger over to him, swish my behind around a little and deliver a big wet lick? He likes it when I do that.

Oh, my! That didn't work either.

Darn it. I can't get a rise out of him, no matter how hard I try. I have rights. I'm part of this family. He can't satisfy me by slipping me a bone once in a while. I need more. I don't like being ignored like this. He's treating me like a dog.

I do have to get him away from that glowing monitor and over here to open this door P.D.Q. (Pretty Darn Quick) — or else.

"Or else what?"

Or else I'll do something terrible.

That's it. I'm at the end of my rope. He's still typing like crazy, still has that glazed look in his eyes, and I'm going nuts because there is a darn squirrel just outside this door on the patio, and I'm squirrel intolerant.

Oh! Oh! He's looking in my direction. Fantastic. I can read his mind. I know what he's thinking. He's going to open the door. Oh, no, he sat back down. Darn.

That's it! I've reached the end of my rope and he still has not opened the door. I'm going lift my leg on his computer tower under the desk.

Such is my dog's life.

Stuff from the Web

The following material came from the *Hollywood Squares* game show and was spontaneous. This TV show, all about fun, had Peter Marshall as the host asking the questions. Many grandkids may not remember this program unless they saw it in reruns.

Q. Do female frogs croak?
A. Paul Lynde: If you hold their little heads under water long enough.

Q. If you're going to make a parachute jump, at least how high should you be?
A. Charley Weaver: Three days of steady drinking should do it.

Q. True or False, a pea can last as long as 5,000 years?
A. George Gobel: Boy, it sure seems that way sometimes.

Q. You've been having trouble going to sleep. Are you probably a man or a woman?
A. Don Knotts: That's what's been keeping me awake.

Q. According to *Cosmopolitan*, if you meet a stranger at a party and you think that he is attractive, is it okay to come out and ask him if he's married?
A. Rose Marie: No, wait until morning.

Q. Which of your five senses tends to diminish as you get older?
A. Charley Weaver: My sense of decency.

WHY DON'T DOGS WEAR SHOES?

Q. In Hawaiian, does it take more than three words to say, "I Love You?"
A. Vincent Price: No, you can say it with a pineapple and a twenty.

Q. What are "Do It," "I Can Help," and "I Can't Get Enough?"
A. George Gobel: I don't know, but it's coming from the next apartment.

Q. As you grow older, do you tend to gesture more or less with your hands while talking?
A. Rose Marie: You ask me one more growing old question, Peter, and I'll give you a gesture you'll never forget.

Q. Paul, why do Hell's Angels wear leather?
A. Because chiffon wrinkles too easily.

Q. Charley, you've just decided to grow strawberries. Are you going to get any during the first year?
A. Charley Weaver: Of course not, I'm too busy growing strawberries.

Q. In bowling, what's a perfect score?
A. Rose Marie: Ralph, the pin boy.

Q. It is considered in bad taste to discuss two subjects at nudist camps. One is politics, what is the other?
A. Paul Lynde: Tape measures.

Q. During a tornado, are you safer in the bedroom or in the closet?
A. Rose Marie: Unfortunately, Peter, I'm always safe in the bedroom.

Q. Can boys join the Camp Fire Girls?
A. Marty Allen: Only after lights out.

Q. When you pat a dog on its head, he will wag his tail. What will a goose do?
A. Paul Lynde: Make him bark?

Q. If you were pregnant for two years, what would you give birth to?
A. Paul Lynde: Whatever it is, it would never be afraid of the dark.

Q. According to Ann Landers, is their anything wrong with getting into the habit of kissing a lot of people?
A. Charley Weaver: It got me out of the army.

Q. While visiting China, your tour guide starts shouting, "Poo! Poo! Poo!" What does this mean?
A. George Gobel: Cattle crossing.

Q. It is the most abused and neglected part of your body, what is it?
A. Paul Lynde: Mine may be abused but it certainly isn't neglected.

Q. Back in the old days, when Great Grandpa put horseradish on his head, what was he trying to do?
A. George Gobel: Get it in his mouth.

Q. Who stays pregnant for a longer period of time, your wife or your elephant?
A. Paul Lynde: Who told you about my elephant?

Q. When a couple has a baby, who is responsible for its sex?
A. Charley Weaver: I'll lend him the car; the rest is up to him.

Q. Jackie Gleason once revealed that he firmly believed in them and had actually seen them on at least two occasions. What are they?
A. Charley Weaver: His feet.

More Doggie Stories

Like people, dogs have special traits within breeds. Here are doggie traits in response to the question, "How many dogs does it take to change a light bulb?"

- Brittany: I'll just stand here stiff like this and point to it so Grandpa Chiappetta can find it and change it.
- German Shorthair: I'll just quiver and look pretty until the Border Collie changes it.
- Golden Retriever: The sun is shining, the day is young, we've got our whole lives ahead of us, and you're inside worrying about a stupid burned-out light bulb?
- Border Collie: Just one? I'll do it and then I'll replace any wiring that's not up to code.
- Dachshund: You know, I can't reach that stupid lamp!
- Toy Poodle: I'll just blow in the Border Collie's ear and he'll do it. By the time he finishes rewiring the house, my nails will be dry. What light bulb?
- Rottweiler: Just try and make me.
- Shih-tzu: Puh-leeze, dah-ling. Let the servants do it.
- Lab: Oh, me, me! Pleeeeeeze let me change the light bulb! Can I? Can I? Huh? Huh? Can I?
- Malamute: Let the Border Collie do it. You can feed me while he's busy.
- Jack Russell Terrier: I'll just pop it in while I'm bouncing off the walls and furniture.
- Cocker Spaniel: Why change it? I can still pee on the carpet in the dark.

- Doberman Pinscher: While it's dark, I'm going to sleep on the couch.
- Boxer: Who cares? I can still play with my squeaky toys in the dark.
- Mastiff: Mastiffs are NOT afraid of the dark.
- Chihuahua: Yo quiero Taco Bulb.
- Irish Wolfhound: Can somebody else do it? I've got this hangover.
- English Pointer: I see it, there it is, there it is, right there.
- Greyhound: If it isn't moving who cares?
- Australian Shepherd: First I'll put all the light bulbs in a little circle.
- Old English Sheep Dog: Light bulb? That thing I just ate was a light bulb?
- Westie: Dogs do not change light bulbs. People change light bulbs. I am not one of THEM, so the question is, how long will it be before I can expect my light?"
- Beagle: If it doesn't smell like a rabbit, forget it.
- Hound Dog: ZZZZZZZZZZZZzzzzzzzzzzzzz.

You can't read these to your grandchild and stay in a sour mood!

1. How do you catch a unique rabbit? Unique up on it.
2. How do you catch a tame rabbit? Tame way. Unique up on it.
3. How do crazy people go through the forest? They take the psycho path.
4. How do you get holy water? You boil the hell out of it.
5. What do fish say when they hit a concrete wall? Dam!
6. What do eskimos get from sitting on the ice too long? Polaroids.
7. What do you call a boomerang that doesn't work? A stick.
8. What do you call cheese that isn't yours? Nacho cheese.
9. What do you call santa's helpers? Subordinate clauses.

WHY DON'T DOGS WEAR SHOES?

10. What do you call four bullfighters in quicksand? Quatro sinko.
11. What do you get from a pampered cow? Spoiled milk.
12. What do you get when you cross a snowman with a vampire? Frostbite.
13. What lies at the bottom of the ocean and twitches? A nervous wreck.
14. What's the difference between roast beef and pea soup? Anyone can roast beef.
15. Where do you find a dog with no legs? Right where you left him.
16. Why do gorillas have big nostrils? Because they have big fingers.
17. Why don't blind people like to skydive? Because it scares the dog.
18. What dind of coffee was served on the Titanic? Sanka.
19. What is the difference between a Harley and a Hoover? The location of the dirt bag.
20. Why did pilgrims' pants always fall down? Because they wore their belt buckles on their hats.
21. What's the difference between a bad golfer and a bad skydiver? A bad golfer goes, "Whack, dang!" A bad skydiver goes, "Dang! Whack."
22. How are a Texas tornado and a Tennessee divorce the same? Somebody's gonna lose a trailer.

A few more of those "YOU KNOW YOU ARE OLD WHEN —"

- Your dreams are reruns.
- The stewardess offers coffee, tea or Milk of Magnesia.
- You sit in a rocking chair and can't get it started.
- Everything you have hurts.
- What doesn't hurt doesn't work.
- You sink your teeth into a juicy steak and they stay there.

A grandfather was at the beach with his grandson when the four-year-old ran up to him, grabbed his hand, and led him to the shore where a seagull was dead on the sand.

"Grandpa, what happened to him?" the boy asked.

"He died and went to Heaven," Grandpa replied.

The boy thought a moment and then said, "Did God throw him back?"

Grab Every Moment

A friend of mine opened his wife's underwear drawer and picked up a silk paper-wrapped package. "This," he said, "isn't any ordinary package." He unwrapped the box and stared at both the silk paper and the box.

"She got this the first time we went to New York eight or nine years ago. She has never put it on because she was saving it for 'a special occasion.' Well, I guess this is it."

He placed the gift box next to the other clothing he was taking to the funeral parlor. His wife had just died.

He turned to me and said, "Never save something for a special occasion. Every day in your life is a special occasion."

Such words can change a life.

Now, as for me, I play more and work less. I visit my family more, fish more in spring and summer and hunt more in the fall and winter. I sit on the porch more without worrying about anything. I play with my dog more than I used to. I spend more time with loved ones, especially the grandkids. I work even less, although I'm supposed to be retired and not working at all.

Life should be a source of experiences to be lived up to, not survived through. I no longer keep anything. I'm giving away more stuff that I like because it makes me feel good.

I'm wearing good shoes and clothes to go to Home Depot, just because I feel like it.

I may buy a car no matter if I hit the lottery or not.

I don't save my special after-shave for special occasions. I use it whenever I want to.

The words "Someday" and "One Day" are fading from my keyboard. If it's worth seeing, listening to or doing it, I want to see it, listen to it or do it now.

I don't know what my friend's wife would have done if she knew she wouldn't be there the next morning. Nobody can tell. I think she might have called relatives and friends. She might call friends to make peace over past quarrels. I'd like to think she would go out for Chinese, her favorite food. It's these small things that I would regret not doing, if I knew my time had come.

I would regret it because I would no longer see my friends or get to write e-mails and other stories I intended to write "one of these days."

I would regret it and feel sad because I didn't say to my mother, my wife, my daughters, my son, my brothers, my sisters and the rest of my extended family how much I love them all.

Even people I don't like, I would like.

Now, I try not to delay, postpone or keep anything that could bring laughter and joy to our lives. And each morning, I say to myself that this could be a special day. Each day, each hour, each minute, is special.

A lot of this philosophy, somebody said, originally came from India, but I doctored it up because I wanted to. Don't keep this to yourself. Make it fit your own life and read it to somebody you care about — or would like to.

Update on a Lifetime Job

Worry about your kids and grandkids never ends.

A decade ago this Grandpa opened his eyes after coronary bypass surgery and there was my mother, in her late seventies at the time, poised with a spoonful of chicken soup ready to feed me. She had driven 350 miles, from Pittsburgh to Detroit, with her bad back to take care of me.

I know of no magic cutoff time when offspring become accountable for their own actions. I know of no wonderful moment when as parents we become detached spectators from the lives of our children and shrug, "It's their life."

When I was in my twenties, I stood in a hospital corridor waiting for doctors to put a few stitches in my son's chin. I asked, "When do you stop worrying?"

A nurse said, "When they get out of the accident stage."

When I was in my thirties, I sat on a little chair in a classroom and heard how one of my kids talked incessantly, disrupted the class, and was headed for a career making license plates. Her teacher said, "Don't worry. They all go through this stage ... and then you can sit back, relax, and enjoy them."

When I was in my forties, I spent a lifetime waiting for the phone to ring, the car to pull into the driveway, the front door to open and my other daughter to come home. A friend said, "They're trying to find themselves. In a few years, you can stop worrying when they're out on dates. They'll be adults."

By the time I was fifty, I was sick and tired of being vulnerable. I was still worrying about my kids, but there was a new wrinkle. There was nothing I could do about it. I continued to anguish over their failures and their disappointments.

We can never stop being parents and for most of us today we can never stop being grandparents.

Friends said that when our kids get married, we might stop worrying and they can lead their own lives. I wanted to believe that but parents are sentenced to a lifetime of worry. Is concern for one another handed down like a torch to blaze the trail of human frailties and the fears of the unknown? Is concern a curse or is it a virtue that elevates us to a higher form of life?

One of my kids became quite irritable recently, saying to me, "Where were you? I've been calling for three days, and no one answered. I was worried."

An elderly Grandma in a Florida retirement home got a call from her son in Chicago.

"How are you?" he asked.

"I've lost some weight," she moaned.

"Been sick?"

"No," she said. "I haven't been eating. Not a thing for a month!"

"Why not, Mom?"

"Because I didn't want to have a mouth full of food in case you called!"

❖ ❖

My forty-something son announced he had given a new girlfriend a diamond ring and planned to marry her. He had been divorced from his first wife for only three months when his e-mail came regarding this new young woman he had just met.

I spent hours drafting a preachy father-to-son e-mail, and then hit the delete key after I re-read it for the tenth time. There wasn't much in the epistle we had not talked about before, and I knew it would accomplish nothing except to upset him and, maybe, drive us apart.

The most important thing I wrote about was not his getting engaged or buying a house or even getting married again. It was about that most frightening, critical thing a kid could do — make you a Grandparent.

Becoming a parent was the hardest thing I had ever done and, in this semi-retired Phase III of my life, I'm still learning about all the things a father can do wrong and how hard it is to do things right. Unfortunately, there is no training or class to enroll in that will transform us into good parents and grandparents. Learning from experience can be brutal for everyone involved.

I wanted to tell my son that in the previous ten years with his former wife, I was happy they did not have children. Neither of them was ready for that step.

There were a lot of stupid people, juveniles, druggies and drunks in the world reproducing at an alarming rate. My son wasn't any one of these, thank God, but he just needed a little seasoning, which he may have by now.

People without brains should be spayed or neutered.

Taking care of a new baby is such an important assignment and so complicated that would-be parents could never dream what they are in for. The one thing for sure is that they are buying into a lifetime job from which they can never resign.

When parenthood hits you between the eyes, your life changes F O R E V E R. You can never go back to being an independent person. You become a "Daddy" or a "Mommy," and then a "Grandpa" or a "Grandma," the stinky diaper-changer, the vomit wiper-upper, live-in baby doctor, and the one who has to answer questions like, "Why don't dogs wear shoes?" or "Who puts the crab in crabapples?"

When you can answer these questions, you might be almost ready to be a Mommy or a Daddy or a Grandpa or a Grandma.

Having a kid isn't like having a pet fish or puppy or cat or bird that you can flush down the toilet or give away or put up on the shelf when you're tired of them. That's it. You've had it. You're a Daddy or Mommy or Grandpa or Grandma for the remainder of your life.

If thoughtful men and women really appreciated the challenge of raising a child (or helping with a grandchild) they might never have unprotected sex again. For those few moments of joy, be prepared for all-night crying, earaches, emergency-room visits, orthodontists, doctor bills, soccer practices, PTA meetings, bruised knees, tears, and all the rest that comes with that territory.

These words are not from one who was tremendously successful as a parent, but from one who has been trying hard to be a good grandparent. These words come from one who has walked that path a few times.

The miracle of my life is that my kids don't all hate me for doing such a poor job of parenting, and that I've got the grandkids tricked into thinking I am neat and cool.

When I opened my eyes and saw my elderly mother trying to spoon-feed me chicken soup in that Detroit hospital more than a decade ago, I realized this woman, who left school in the tenth grade for an arranged marriage, knew what the hell parenthood was all about.

My mother was doing what good parents have to do — fulfill a job that never ends.

Good luck. Now, go love those kids.

The End